# CRANKY

**Based on *The Railway Series* by the Rev. W. Awdry**

Illustrations by
*Robin Davies and Jerry Smith*

EGMONT

First published in Great Britain 2003
by Egmont Books Limited
239 Kensington High Street, London W8 6SA
All Rights Reserved

Thomas the Tank Engine & Friends

A BRITT ALLCROFT COMPANY PRODUCTION

Based on The Railway Series by The Rev W Awdry

© Gullane (Thomas) LLC 2003

ISBN 1 4052 0698 5
10
Printed in Great Britain

*This is a story about Cranky the Crane. He worked at the Docks on the Island of Sodor. He played tricks on the engines, to get them into trouble. But one day Cranky needed the engines' help …*

Thomas and Percy liked working at the Docks. So when The Fat Controller told them they would be working there for two weeks, they could hardly wait. But when they arrived at the Docks, there was a new crane there called Cranky. Cranky was always moody and he called Thomas and Percy 'useless little bugs'.

The two engines were very upset. They told Gordon and James about how rude Cranky had been. To their surprise, James and Gordon backed up Cranky.

"He's so high up in the air," said James, "facing the wind, rain and sunshine, that it's no wonder he looks down and sees you as annoying little bugs!"

Thomas and Percy hoped Cranky would stop being so mean to them.

The next day, Cranky played a trick on Thomas. He told him to move the trucks to the outer track. Thomas was surprised, but he did as he was told.

When The Fat Controller arrived, Cranky said, "I asked Thomas to put those trucks on the inner track, but he has put them on the outer track, where I can't reach them. And Percy won't do as he's told, either!"

The Fat Controller was furious. He sent the engines back to the station in disgrace. Thomas and Percy were shocked. Cranky was making it all up!

A storm raged across the Island of Sodor that night. At The Fat Controller's station, Thomas and Percy talked about Cranky. They were upset that The Fat Controller had believed his lies. They wondered if they'd ever be allowed to work at the Docks again.

"If Cranky is going to continue being nasty to us then I don't want to work at the Docks anyway!" Thomas said.

Percy had to agree.

At the Docks, the wind and rain was lashing down on Cranky. He wasn't worried though – he thought he was much stronger than any storm.

In the shed nearby, Duck, James and Gordon were listening to the storm. They thought they were safe there, but they were wrong. A huge steamer had got loose and it was heading straight for the Docks!

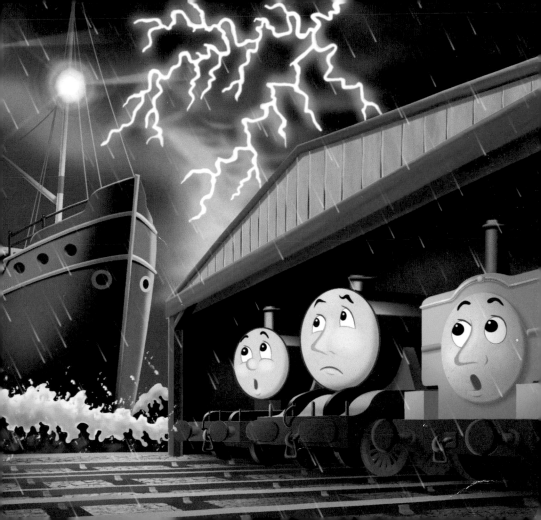

The steamer ran aground. It charged through the Docks, crashing into the shed and knocking over Cranky.

Duck, Gordon and James were trapped! They called to Cranky for help but Cranky had fallen on to his side, so he needed rescuing, too!

Cranky and the engines had to wait for the storm to clear before they could be rescued.

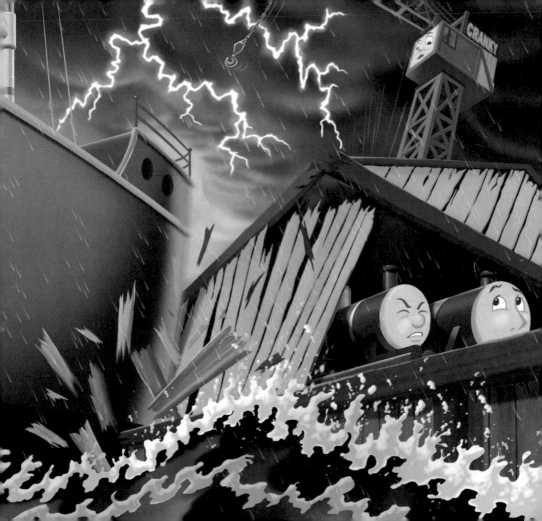

The next morning, The Fat Controller went to the Docks.

"Thomas and Percy are coming to help you, Cranky," he said. "They'll have you up again in no time!"

"Oh, thank you!" said Cranky. "Erm, can you tell them I'm sorry that I was so mean to them?"

"So it was you that was causing all the trouble?" said The Fat Controller. "It seems I owe those engines an apology."

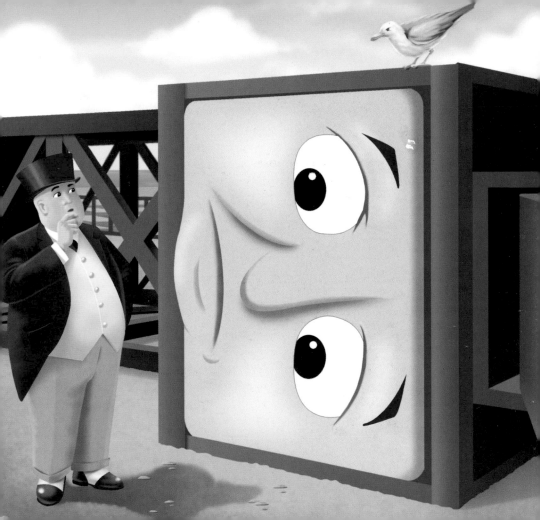

Thomas and Percy's Drivers tied ropes to Cranky and attached them to the engines. Thomas and Percy quickly pulled Cranky back upright.

Cranky was very glad to see the world the right way up again. He got straight to work, clearing away the rubble.

Cranky moved the steamer back into the water and it was carefully tied in place. Then it was safe for him to pull the heavy rubble away from the shed so the trapped engines could get out.

Duck, Gordon and James were very grateful. They had not liked being stuck in the shed. They thanked Cranky for his help.

Cranky told them Thomas and Percy had rescued him first.

"I never thought I'd be rescued by a couple of ..." Cranky was about to say 'bugs', but he stopped himself just in time. "Erm," he continued, "I never thought I would be saved by a couple of small engines! I'll try not to be rude to you again."

Thomas and Percy smiled. They were just about to reply when Cranky said, "Now move out of the way, you mites, I need to get to those trucks!"

"Pah!" said Percy. "Cranky wasn't polite for long – he's back to bugging us!"

Percy quickly moved up the track to get out of Cranky's way, but he had forgotten that his ropes were still attached to Cranky.

"Wait!" cried Thomas, but he was too late. As Percy charged forward, the ropes pulled taut and Cranky crashed back to the ground with a THUMP!

Thomas and Percy had to pull Cranky up for the second time. Cranky felt very silly.

Now Cranky works well with Thomas and Percy. He still looks down on them from his high perch in the sky, but he never calls them bugs or mites. After that stormy night, he knows they can be Really Useful Engines; after all, they had rescued him twice! And if Cranky is ever knocked over again, he knows the little engines will quickly put him back in his place.

**The Thomas Story Library is THE definitive collection of stories about Thomas and ALL his Friends.**

5 more Thomas Story Library titles will be chuffing into your local bookshop in Summer 2006:

**Fergus**
**Mighty Mac**
**Harvey**
**Rusty**
**Molly**

And there are even more
Thomas Story Library books to follow later!
**So go on, start your Thomas Story Library NOW!**

## A Fantastic Offer for Thomas the Tank Engine Fans!

In every Thomas Story Library book like this one, you will find a special token. Collect 6 Thomas tokens and we will send you a brilliant Thomas poster, and a double-sided bedroom door hanger!
Simply tape a £1 coin in the space above, and fill out the form overleaf.

## TO BE COMPLETED BY AN ADULT

To apply for this great offer, ask an adult to complete the coupon below and send it with a pound coin and 6 tokens, to:

THOMAS OFFERS, PO BOX 715, HORSHAM RH12 5WG

☐ Please send a Thomas poster and door hanger. I enclose 6 tokens plus a £1 coin. (Price includes P&P)

Fan's name.................................................................................

Address....................................................................................

..........................................................Postcode...............................

Date of birth................................................................................

Name of parent/guardian.................................................................

Signature of parent/guardian.............................................................